PRINCESS CharmSCHOOL

Adapted by Gabrielle Reyes
Based on the screenplay by Elise Allen
Illustrated by Ulkutay Design Group

SCHOLASTIC INC.

New York   Toronto   London   Auckland

Sydney   Mexico City   New Delhi   Hong Kong

ISBN 978-0-545-33311-5

12 11 10 9 8 7 6 5 4 3 2 1   11 12 13 14 15 16/0
Printed in the U.S.A.   40
First printing, October 2011

Special thanks to Vicki Jaeger, Monica Okazaki, Ann McNeill, Emily Kelly, Sharon Woloszyk, Julia Phelps, Tanya Mann, Rob Hudnut, David Wiebe, Shelley Dvi-Vardhana, Michelle Cogan, Rainmaker Entertainment, Walter P. Martishius, Carla Alford, Rita Lichtwardt, Kathy Berry, and Miranda Nolte.

Chapter 1

Emily sat at the kitchen table with piles of homework in front of her. She adjusted the paper tiara on her head as she stared at the television.

"Welcome back, everyone!" said the news announcer. "Andrea and I are thrilled to be presenting the one hundred forty-fourth Princess Procession!"

"Yes, Phil. It's so exciting to see the princesses-to-be arriving on their first

day at Princess Charm School!" added Andrea, the other newscaster.

Even with the fuzzy TV reception, Emily could see how happy the girls were as they descended one by one from the horse-drawn carriages.

"Yes, every girl dreams it, but only those who are part of royal families in kingdoms far and wide can attend the school to earn their princess crowns," Phil continued.

"As always, joining the class of princesses-to-be are the lucky few who are part of a special category. They are not from royal lineage, but they attend Princess Charm School with the princesses. After graduation, each girl hopes to win a position as a princess's most trusted advisor, a lady royal!" Andrea explained.

"You'll hurt your royal eyes looking at that, Emily," joked a tall girl from the front doorway.

"Blair, you're home!" shouted Emily. "Let me get you a tiara!"

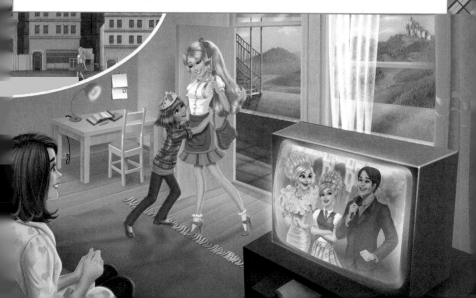

Blair pulled a pink bobby pin from the pocket of her waitress uniform and used it to fiddle with the back of the TV. The reception cleared up perfectly just as Emily set a paper tiara on Blair's head. "How's Mom?" Blair asked her little sister.

"I'm just fine."

Blair turned to see her mother coming into the room wearing a tired smile. She set the handle of her cane on the table and sat down between her daughters. "How was work today, Blair?"

"It was good, Mom," Blair answered. She reached into her uniform pockets and dropped handfuls of coins into a plastic jar. "We'll have enough money to move into a new house AND get you the best doctors . . ." Blair looked at the half-full jar. ". . . eventually."

"It's time for the lottery drawing!" Emily squealed, her eyes glued to the TV screen.

The newscasters explained the Princess Charm School's annual lottery in which one regular citizen of the kingdom of Gardania could win a full scholarship to the school and the chance to become a princess's lady royal after graduation.

Blair and her mother turned their attention to Emily. "When you're old enough, we'll enter you. I promise," Blair said as she adjusted her sister's tiara.

"And this year's lottery winner is . . ." said a voice from the TV.

Emily crossed her fingers and closed her eyes.

". . . Blair Willows."

"Yes!" Emily shrieked as she leaped out

of her seat and gave a crushing hug to her stunned sister.

"Emily!" cried Blair. "You entered my name in the lottery?!"

"Only . . . five or six times a day . . . for the last year!" Emily was still in the middle of dancing around the kitchen table when the doorbell rang. "They're here!" she shouted and ran to open the apartment door.

A towering man named Brock stood in front of the door. "Blair Willows?" he asked flatly. "I'm here to take you to Princess Charm School."

"I'm sorry, but there's been a mistake," said Blair. She turned to Emily. "Look at me! I don't belong in a school with a bunch of princesses! And you guys need me here!"

"It wasn't right of Emily to go behind your back . . . but this is a big opportunity," Blair's mother said. "A position as a lady royal . . ." she started to say.

". . . would change our lives forever," Blair finished. She sighed. "Okay . . . I'll go. But I'm only doing it for the two of you," she whispered as she looked down at her stained waitress uniform. "I am *so* not a princess. . . ."

Chapter 2

Before Blair knew it, she and Brock were pulling up to Princess Charm School in a horse and carriage. Blair had no idea what to expect as she walked into the school's massive entranceway. She had barely stepped inside the door when something came out of nowhere and knocked her to the ground.

"Whoa! Easy there," Blair said to the big golden retriever licking her face. She patted the happy dog and looked at

the heart-shaped tag hanging from his collar. "This says your name is Prince. You sure are friendly, Prince."

"Not usually," said a woman's voice. "And we usually don't find our future lady royals rolling around on the floor, either." Blair rushed to her feet immediately. She recognized the woman standing in front of her from the TV broadcast of the Princess

Procession. It was Headmistress Privet, the one in charge of Princess Charm School.

Privet looked Blair up and down. "You must be Blair Willows. Welcome to Princess Charm School, Blair." Privet began to walk down the hall at a brisk pace and gestured for Blair to follow. "This way," she said as she pushed through some double doors.

Privet pointed out various classrooms, the cafeteria, and the luxury spa. Then Blair heard a tiny voice calling, "Blair Willows? I'm looking for a Blair Willows—oof!" A tiny winged sprite slammed right into Blair.

"And finally, this is Grace." Privet explained, "Every student has a sprite who is her personal princess assistant. Grace will begin by showing you to your locker." And with that, the headmistress walked away.

"At your service, Miss Willows!" Grace said excitedly. "Let's go to your locker so you can change clothes. Right this way!"

Grace flew over to a locker and struggled to open it. "Let's see. I am always forgetting this . . . uh . . . sixty-five, thirty-two, forty-one? No. Sixteen, fifteen, eight! No . . . oh! Three, nine, fifty-nine? Woo-hoo! Got it!" Suddenly, the door burst open, revealing not only books and school supplies but also gem-colored mirrors, a collection of cosmetics, and a row of fashionable high-heeled shoes.

"I can't believe this is my locker!" Blair said with a smile.

"And there's more! We've got a jewel-crusted hairbrush, diamond lipstick, and, oh, this perfume that I love," Grace exclaimed as she took each item out of the locker and tossed it to Blair. When Blair caught the perfume, she accidentally squeezed the bottle and squirted a very pretty girl who was walking down the hallway.

"UGH!"

"Uh-oh . . ." Grace whispered.

"Oh! I'm so sorry!" cried Blair. "It was an accident—"

"How dare you! Do you know who I am?!" shouted the girl. "I am the future princess of Gardania and now I REEK of terrible perfume!"

"Uh . . . I just got here and . . . I'm new to all of this. . . ." Blair stammered.

The future princess of Gardania checked out Blair from head to toe. "Let me guess. You're Blair Willows from the lottery. Well, let me tell you something. Commoners like you don't belong here. So do yourself a favor and leave before you make a total fool out of yourself." She then stormed down the hall and yelled to her sprite, "Get me a Princess Pamper Package PRONTO!"

"Uh . . . that was Delancy," said Grace, who had been hiding behind Blair. "And that's her personal princess assistant, Wickellia. As you can see, everyone here is very nice . . . most of the time. Let's get you into your uniform. Locker, please extend the curtain for a Princess Primp."

13

Blair stared at the curtain as it opened up.

"Oh, it's fabulous! The best thing about Princess Charm School! Get gorgeous!" Grace said happily.

Blair walked over to the curtain, which soon closed around her. When the curtain opened just a moment later, Blair found herself standing in a Princess Charm School uniform.

"Pretty as a princess, er, lady royal. Now let's get you settled in your new room," said Grace.

A few minutes later, Blair was admiring her stunning new bedroom. Her roommates, Hadley and Isla, who were both princesses-in-training, had made Blair feel at home right away. Blair told the girls about her first meeting with Delancy.

"Well, if you think Delancy's bad, just wait until you meet her mom, Dame Devin," said Hadley.

Isla explained, "Dame Devin is a teacher at Princess Charm School. She says that this is her last year teaching, since Delancy will be taking over the kingdom of Gardania when she gets crowned a princess at the end of the year."

"According to Dame Devin, no one knows the palace and the royal life like *she* does. She's lived at the palace ever since her sister-in-law, Queen Isabella, and her family died in an accident years ago . . ." Hadley continued.

". . . *if* they died," Hadley and Isla

muttered in unison. Hadley and Isla exchanged a knowing look. "I *so* love that you know this legend, too!" Hadley said with a smile.

Blair listened curiously as her roommates explained the rumor of Queen Isabella and Gardania's magical crown. It was said that there was a magical crown in the kingdom of Gardania that would light up when placed upon the true heir of the kingdom. It lit up on Queen Isabella's coronation, but the crown hadn't been seen since her accident. According to another rumor in the kingdom, some of Queen Isabella's family members were still alive. Some thought these family members were kept as prisoners in the palace dungeons.

"Wow, my sister would love these stories," said Blair.

"They're not just stories!" the two roommates said at the exact same time. Hadley and Isla looked at each other and laughed.

"We'd better get to the Starlight Welcome," said Hadley. "We don't want to upset Headmistress Privet and Dame Devin. They might put *us* in the palace dungeon!"

Chapter 3

The next day, Blair stood nervously in her first class. At the previous night's Starlight Welcome, Headmistress Privet had made it clear that making it to graduation would be hard work. Blair ran through a checklist of Privet's rules in her head: *Attend every class on time and in uniform. Work hard and stay dedicated to keep up good grades.*

She was in uniform and arrived at her class on time. Now all she had to do was work hard. Too bad Blair felt like she had no idea what she was doing. She stood in a line with the other lady-royals-in-training while Isla and Hadley stood on the other side of the room with the class of princesses-in-training.

"Proper poise is a necessity for anyone living a royal life," said Dame Devin as she handed each girl one book. "Now, let's start with one book on your head and see how gracefully you can glide across the room."

Blair looked around the room and saw Delancy walking toward her with ten books balanced on her head. Delancy glared at Blair as she passed by.

Blair put the book on her head and tried to move forward without letting it fall. She was concentrating so hard that she didn't see Delancy stick her foot out in front of her. *CRASH!*

Blair tripped over Delancy's foot and went flying. She tried to catch herself by grabbing on to Isla nearby. The two of them landed on the floor at the same time as both their books slammed on the ground with a loud thump.

"Stand up this instant!" Dame Devin commanded. She crossed the room in three quick steps and stood over the two girls while Delancy smirked in the background.

"It was an accident," Blair tried to

explain as she got back on her feet.

"You're the lottery girl, aren't you?" Dame Devin asked. "Look at me, girl. A true lady royal never hangs her head." Blair raised her head to meet Dame Devin's gaze. When their eyes met, Dame Devin gasped. She couldn't stop staring at Blair's eyes.

"Mother!" hissed Delancy, snapping Dame Devin out of her shock.

Dame Devin's face flushed an angry red. "You . . . are unfit for royal life! I want you out of this class!" Dame Devin said.

"I un-understand," stammered Blair, her cheeks burning hot as she left the classroom.

Blair's first week only got worse. When she stood up to take away her tray in the cafeteria, she somehow ended up dragging the tablecloth — and the trays of all the other students at her table — with her! All of the trays fell to the ground while food got all over Blair's uniform. She had embarrassed herself in front of the whole school.

"Who am I kidding?" Blair moaned to Hadley and Isla that night in their room. "Dame Devin is right. I'm not Princess Charm School material."

"You have to give yourself more time," said Isla comfortingly.

Hadley was about to agree with Isla when she was interrupted by a knock on the door.

"A little help, please?" said Grace.

Hadley opened the door to find Grace struggling with a huge box. "Care package for Blair. It says it's from Emily," Grace said as she dropped the box on Blair's bed.

"My little sister!" Blair said as she began to tear open the box.

Inside she found a paper tiara and pictures that Emily had drawn. Blair held up one of the drawings with care. "Emily loves the story of how I was found on my mom's doorstep. I was only one," Blair explained. "Mom took me in right away, and she adopted Emily a few years later. . . . The two of them are everything to me." Blair set the drawing on the bed and picked up the paper tiara. "It's hard for me here . . . but I have to stay for my mom and for my sister."

Everyone was so wrapped up in looking at Emily's drawings that no one noticed that Headmistress Privet had been standing outside their bedroom door listening in.

Chapter 4

The next day, Blair, Hadley, and Isla had social dancing class taught by Headmistress Privet. Blair was no better at dancing than she was at book balancing. She kept stepping on her partners' toes and stumbling into other dancers. But she didn't stop trying. When Headmistress Privet asked her to stay for a few minutes after class, she braced herself for bad news.

"Blair . . ." Privet began but wasted no time getting to the point. "Dame Devin recommended we send you home."

Blair's heart sank. "Oh . . ."

"I can't say I blame her. You've been a disaster ever since you got here. Last night, I was almost going to do it. . . ." Privet paused and studied her student. "Blair, do you know what makes a princess?"

Blair thought for a second. "A crown?"

"No," Privet continued. "Character and confidence make a princess. All of our classes in poise, manners, accessorizing, and dancing are supposed to build confidence. You have character . . . but no confidence."

"I see . . . well . . . thank you for the opportunity and—" Blair faltered.

"I'm not finished," said Privet. "I'm not going to expel you, Blair. I realize you want to work hard and you have a lot of potential. So instead, I'm going to tutor you."

Blair could hardly believe what she heard. "You . . . you're going to help . . . me?"

Privet nodded. She didn't like to repeat herself. Blair rushed over and gave her a huge hug.

"Rule number one: No hugging the tutor," the headmistress said with a small smile.

"Uh . . . sorry. I just couldn't help it." Blair smiled widely. "When do we start?"

Blair and Headmistress Privet spent hours after school each day working on Blair's poise, balance, and manners while Prince the dog watched attentively. Privet modeled standing on one foot on a branch of a tree while holding beautiful potted orchid plants in each hand. She explained that she was able to find balance anywhere because she was comfortable in her own body.

"No one can make you feel inferior without your consent," Privet explained.

After months of hard work, Blair's performance in her classes started to improve. She could glide with twenty books atop her head. She moved around comfortably in elaborate, sparkling gowns. She was able to dance without leaving her partners with bruised toes. And she even started to enjoy herself.

One morning, Blair, Hadley, and Isla were on their way to ballroom dance class when they overheard their classmates chatting excitedly. "They're here! The princes are here!"

When the girls entered the classroom, they saw their classmates standing in small groups on one side of the room. On the other side, a class of princes-to-be stood together.

"Welcome to our surprise joint dance class with the students from Prince Charming Academy," Headmistress Privet said. "Now let's begin. I need two rows: Ladies, stand on the pink line. Gentlemen, stand on the blue line."

While the other girls found their places in line, Delancy turned to her friend Portia. "I don't see Prince Nicholas," Delancy whispered. "I've had a crush on him forever. I *have* to be the one to dance with him!"

"It seems that there is one extra girl, so

whoever doesn't have a partner can sit and watch," Headmistress Privet instructed.

Dame Devin noticed her daughter standing apart from the others. She hurried over, grabbed her by the arm, and dragged her to the line. "No daughter of mine sits on the sidelines," she said. After making sure Headmistress Privet was looking the other way, Dame Devin pushed Blair out of line and shoved Delancy into Blair's spot.

"But Mother!" Delancy protested.

"All right! We're ready to begin!" Dame Devin called out to Headmistress Privet. She gestured to Blair and said, "Looks like you're going to have to sit this one out, dear," and pointed to some empty chairs by the door.

Blair started to head toward the chairs when the door burst open.

"Wait! Sorry I'm so late—"

Smash!

A new boy had run into the room—and right into Blair! Both of them fell to the ground.

Delancy gasped. It was Prince Nicholas!

"Oh no! I'm so sorry!" the prince said as he rushed to get up on his feet. "Please let me help you." He extended his hand.

"Oh, I'm okay," Blair said. Suddenly, she felt the whole room of students looking at her. Wanting to do the right thing, she accepted his hand. Prince Nicholas met Blair's eyes and was immediately struck by her beauty. When Blair looked into his eyes, she felt herself blush. "Um . . . thank you," she said softly.

Delancy's cheeks turned red with anger as she watched Privet guide Prince Nicholas and Blair to positions in line opposite each other.

"Well then, I will excuse your lateness so that everyone can have a partner," Privet said. "*Now* let's begin. Princes, please introduce yourselves politely and lightly kiss the top of your partners' hands."

Blair extended her hand to Nicholas.

"M'lady," Nicholas began with a playful and overly flowery tone. "I am Nicholas, a young swain most privileged to make your acquaintance." He kissed Blair's hand. "Think that was polite enough?" he asked, returning to his normal voice.

"Absolutely," Blair said. "But I can top it." She curtseyed, then said, "I, kind sir, am Blair, maiden of Gardania, and am honored to be welcomed into your swainy company."

Privet turned on the music and instructed the princes to take the lead. Nicholas raised his arm and gently laid his hand on Blair's back. Blair spun elegantly under his arm and they swayed across the floor. Their dancing was flawless.

"I can't believe I'm not falling all over the place," Blair said. "I was a disaster of a dancer when I first got here. I'm only here because I won the lottery...."

Nicholas looked into her eyes as they danced. "That's funny . . . I feel like I won the lottery, too."

Blair felt warmth in her cheeks. Before she could respond, Headmistress Privet called out, "Wonderful, everyone! Now make a final bow and say farewell. You'll see each other again at the Coronation Day ceremony."

Nicholas bowed. "I will count the moments till then, m'lady," he said, putting on the flowery voice again.

Blair laughed. "As will I, good sir." She beamed and gave Nicholas one last smile before he joined the other boys exiting the classroom.

After ballroom dance class, the students were given the rest of the day off to

prepare for a special etiquette class and
dinner at the palace. Headmistress Privet
told all of her students to get pampered
at the spa.

After a lovely afternoon, Blair, Hadley,
and Isla returned to their room to get ready.
The girls gasped when they went inside and
noticed that their uniforms were cut to
shreds.

Blair cried, "Our uniforms are ruined!"

Isla shook her head in disbelief. "What are we going to do? We're not allowed in class without our uniforms."

Hadley sadly added, "And if we skip a class, we get an F."

"We can't fail! We are almost done. Coronation Day is on Saturday!" said Blair. "How could this happen?"

"Seriously, it was Delancy," Hadley replied. "It had to be. She loves to make you feel inferior, Blair."

Blair thought for a moment about what Hadley said. She felt hurt and defeated by Delancy. But then she remembered one of the lessons Headmistress Privet had taught her. "*No one can make you feel inferior, not without your consent,*" Blair thought. Then she looked at her friends and smiled. She had an idea!

Chapter 5

Later that night, Dame Devin and Headmistress Privet stood at the door to the palace and watched all of the students arrive. Dame Devin said with a satisfied smile, "It seems Blair, Hadley, and Isla are running late. I do hope they're not skipping class. I'd hate to fail anyone so close to Coronation Day." When the last student walked through the door to the palace, Dame Devin looked at her watch and said, "Well, time's up."

Headmistress Privet replied, "I think we can wait a few more minutes."

"And keep the other students waiting?" asked Dame Devin. "That hardly seems fair. I'm afraid we'll have to fail all three of them." She started to close the door.

"Wait!" cried Blair as she, Hadley, and Isla raced to the palace. The girls were wearing fabulous personalized versions of their uniforms!

As the girls reached the castle, Dame Devin scolded, "What do you think you're wearing? Those aren't school-issued uniforms!"

"Actually, they are made entirely from the material in our original uniforms," Blair explained.

"That's against the rules!" Dame Devin replied angrily.

Headmistress Privet smiled. "Actually, there is nothing in the dress code against what they've done."

"Right. We just used some hard work to unlock our princess potential," said Blair.

"And beautifully, at that. Come join the class," Headmistress Privet said as she opened the door wider so that the girls could enter the palace.

Blair, Hadley, and Isla joined their classmates in the grand foyer of the palace. The classmates excitedly asked the three girls about their cool uniforms.

After a few minutes, the headmistress clapped for everyone's attention, and the girls quieted down. Privet explained that the students would have time to explore the first floor of the palace before dinner. Delancy watched Blair, Isla, and Hadley break into a group by themselves. She watched them as they walked down an ornate hallway lined with portraits and began to secretly follow them.

Isla was studying the beautiful curved shape of the ceiling when something on the wall caught her eye.

"Blair!" she cried. "Blair, Hadley! Look!" she said, pointing to a painting. The

girls followed her finger and saw a portrait of a girl who looked exactly like Blair. She was wearing a sparkly crown and a beautiful royal gown.

Blair was speechless. This didn't make any sense. She had never had her portrait painted and she had never even been to the palace. She read the nameplate below the painting. "'Princess Isabella, age eighteen.' That's my age!"

Isla pointed to the next painting. "Look at this one!" The painting was of an older blond woman holding a baby and standing with a handsome man. Snuggling up next to the family was a golden retriever puppy wearing a very familiar heart-shaped tag.

Isla read the nameplate. "Queen Isabella, King Reginald, Princess Sophia, and their loyal dog . . . Prince." Then she asked, "Blair . . . *when* did your mom find you on her doorstep?"

"The date? It was April twenty-sixth. She didn't know my real birthday, so that day became my birthday. The doctor said I looked about a year old then. . . ."

Her roommates both whipped out their cell phones and began typing. "Got it!" Hadley called as she looked up from her phone. "April twenty-sixth was the day that the royal family died in the car crash!"

Blair could barely hear what her roommates were trying to say. Hadley and Isla kept interrupting each other as they pointed out all of the coincidences: Blair was a year old when she was found on her mother's doorstep; Princess Sophia was a year old at the time of the car crash; Prince, the school's dog, adored Blair; and Blair looked just like Queen Isabella.

"Blair!" Hadley exclaimed. "*You* could be Princess Sophia!"

"And that would explain why Dame Devin and Delancy are so awful to you. They know *you're* the rightful heir to the throne — not Delancy!" Isla burst out.

Blair thought for sure that she was the one most in shock. But she, Isla, and Hadley didn't realize that Delancy was listening from around the corner. Delancy was completely stunned.

A moment passed before Blair started laughing. "Okay, wait. This is crazy. If I really *were* Princess Sophia, that would make Dame Devin my aunt and . . . and . . . Delancy would . . . be . . . my cousin!"

"Ew!" the three roommates cried.

Just then they heard a bell ringing.

"Blair, you know we're not kidding about this, right?" Hadley asked.

"This is serious! The whole fate of

Gardania is at stake!" Isla exclaimed.

Blair rolled her eyes. "Come on, you guys, it's time for dinner. We can't be late."

As they left to head to dinner, they passed Delancy, who had ducked behind a huge tapestry. Once the three girls were out of sight, Delancy hurried over to look at the portraits. She realized that the girls were right. The young Princess Isabella looked just like Blair!

Chapter 6

The palace dinner passed by in a blur. Delancy couldn't pay attention to anything around her. She couldn't get the image of Queen Isabella and baby Sophia out of her mind. *Could someone really have left a baby on a stranger's doorstep? And could it have been my very own mother?* Her thoughts were interrupted only when her mother made a shocking announcement. Dame Devin told the assembled students and teachers that once Delancy was crowned princess the following week, she would be destroying the buildings on the outskirts of the kingdom and replacing them with parks and gardens.

Blair couldn't believe what she was hearing. She immediately stood up.

"People live in those areas!" Blair exclaimed. "My family and I live there! Where will people go?"

Dame Devin replied, "They'll move. . . . Nearby kingdoms can extend charity by taking in people without homes!" She gestured to Blair but avoided looking at her. "If you're concerned about your family, I would leave school immediately and prepare them to move. Delancy's plan will take place the minute she's crowned, so you don't have much time."

Blair then looked from Dame Devin

to Delancy. "You wouldn't really do this, would you?"

Delancy was speechless. As she looked at Blair's face, her mind flashed back to the portrait of the young Princess Sophia. She soon realized that her mother's plan would leave Blair's family homeless. Delancy had no idea how to respond. "I have nothing to say," she finally muttered.

Blair held her gaze a moment longer, then turned and left the room. Seconds

47

later, Hadley and Isla left to find her.

With Blair out of sight, Delancy turned to her mother. "I was in the hall of portraits," Delancy started. "I saw a painting of Queen Isabella when she was young . . . and I see the way you are with Blair. . . ." She paused. "Does it have anything to do with her being baby Sophia?" she asked.

Dame Devin looked surprised but recovered quickly. She looked deep into her daughter's eyes and asked, "Do you really want to know the answer?"

Delancy opened her mouth, sure of her response. But when her eyes met Dame Devin's ice-cold glare, suddenly Delancy was afraid of the horrible things her mother could have done and could still do.

She closed her mouth.

Dame Devin nodded. "I didn't think so."

48

"Blair must have left the palace," Isla said as she and Hadley made their way down the hall.

"We need to find her," said Hadley. The friends headed back to the school. After some searching, the duo saw Blair with her head down in the school quad.

"Oh, Blair, don't cry," said Isla. "It'll all be okay."

Blair looked up to face her friends. There were no tears on her face—only a determined smile. "Oh, I'm better than okay," Blair told them. "I'm ready."

Hadley asked, "Does this mean you believe us?"

"Delancy can't be crowned the princess of Gardania if we can prove that someone else, possibly me, is the rightful heir to the kingdom," Blair declared. "We need to find that magical crown—tonight!"

Later that night, Blair and her roommates waited until the other students were asleep. But just as they were ready to leave the room, a loud alarm blared.

"It's the fire alarm!" the three roommates heard a girl shout from outside their door.

The girls headed into the hall and joined the sleepy students Dame Devin was directing. When Dame Devin saw Delancy at the end of the line, she pulled her aside. "You're staying with me," she whispered.

Dame Devin dragged Delancy back down the hall to Blair's room.

"You keep watch," she told her daughter. She ducked into the room and shut the door. Moments later she stepped back out.

Delancy stared at her mother. "Mom . . . what did you do?"

"Nothing for you to worry about," her mother said. "You have your big Coronation Day to think about. Let's join the others outside."

Delancy looked at Blair's door once more, and then followed her mother down the hall.

It turned out to be a false alarm. Once the fire trucks left, the students all returned to their rooms. Blair, Hadley, and Isla decided to wait until everyone was back in bed before trying to sneak out of the palace. Blair was putting some things they'd need into her backpack when she was startled by shouting outside the door.

"Thieves!" Dame Devin cried. "They're thieves, I tell you!"

A moment later, Dame Devin, Brock, Headmistress Privet, and Delancy barged into their bedroom. Dame Devin was insisting that the girls be arrested for stealing her jewelry.

"What?!?" Blair said with disbelief. "But I would never do something like that!"

"Not even to save your poor, poor family from losing their home?" Dame Devin said accusingly. "It doesn't matter what you say because Delancy saw you." Dame Devin looked at her daughter pointedly. "Isn't that right, Delancy?"

Delancy's eyes darted from Blair to her mother. "I . . . I don't remember," she stammered. Then she saw her mother's eyes narrow and feared what her mother would do to her. "I . . . Yes. Yes, I did."

Headmistress Privet had no choice but to have Brock search the room. Blair, Hadley, and Isla stood helplessly as they watched Brock look through each of their desks, drawers, and closets.

"Got it!" he said as he withdrew his hand from underneath Blair's mattress. He held up a beautiful diamond necklace. Brock then found necklaces hidden underneath both Hadley's and Isla's mattresses, too.

All the girls were shocked. Blair ran over to Headmistress Privet. "We didn't

steal any of this!" she cried.

Headmistress Privet sighed. "I'm afraid with the evidence we see here and Delancy as a witness, I have to take this seriously. With the coronation ceremony just a few hours away, Brock will take you to the detaining rooms where you will be held until I can investigate this in the morning."

"Detained? As in locked up? And miss the coronation?" Hadley looked like she had been slapped.

"I'm afraid so," Privet replied. Then she gave Delancy a look and said, "Unless there's another way to explain this . . ."

Delancy swallowed hard but said nothing.

Privet looked disappointed but gave a nod. Brock handcuffed the girls and led them out of the room to lock them up.

Chapter 7

"Hadley . . . Isla . . . I'm so sorry!" Blair cried as Brock led the three of them down the hallway. "Now neither of you will become princesses!"

"Who needs a crown anyway?" Hadley tried to joke. "They just make your head itch—"

"STOP!" Brock froze and the girls whipped their heads around. Who was that?

It was Delancy walking quickly toward them. In a commanding voice, Delancy said, "Brock, I have a new plan for the prisoners. You are to turn them over to me."

Brock looked hesitant. "But my orders . . ."

"Your orders will officially come from me in a few hours. *If* you still have a job once I'm crowned princess," she warned.

Brock scanned Delancy's face and saw she was serious. "They're all yours," he said as he handed Delancy the keys to the detaining room and the handcuffs.

Once Brock was gone, Delancy turned to Blair, Hadley, and Isla. "I don't have a lot of time," she whispered as she quickly unlocked their handcuffs. "Tell me—" she asked as she freed Blair. "Are you really Princess Sophia?"

Blair blinked with surprise. "I . . . I don't know for sure . . . but I think so. Yes."

Delancy looked her in the eye. "I think

so, too." She thought for a moment and then grabbed a piece of paper from a nearby table. She started drawing furiously. "This is a map of the palace basement and vault area," she explained. "Something that belongs to you is inside the vault."

"Do you mean . . . Gardania's magical crown?" asked Blair.

"You have to find it so everyone can know the truth," Delancy replied.

Blair didn't understand. "But . . . that means you won't be crowned the princess of Gardania."

"I want what's right," Delancy said seriously.

"I . . ." Blair had no idea what to say. "Thank you, Delancy."

Delancy nodded. She explained as much as she could about the map she had drawn and then handed it to Blair. "I have to get back so my mother doesn't suspect anything. Now go! Hurry!"

The girls looked at one another and thanked Delancy. "We're going to need my wonderful sprite, Grace, to help us, too," Blair said. Then they hurried down the hallway. Delancy watched them go.

The three roommates and Grace studied the map Delancy had drawn. A few minutes later, the girls had successfully climbed through a window, thanks to Grace's expert flying skills, and crept as quietly as they could down a short hall. Grace flew in behind them.

The girls got into the freight elevator, which took them down to a small basement chamber. As Delancy had drawn on the map, there was a door with a big handle on the far wall. "That has to be the door to the vault," Blair said.

"Don't move!" Hadley whispered as she pointed to a blinking red light. "Laser alarm. There must be lasers all over the room." Blair and Isla gave her a confused look. "If we get in the way of any beams, an alarm will go off," Hadley explained.

The girls were stumped. How were they supposed to figure out where the beams were? "I've got an idea," said Blair. She pulled a jar of face powder out of her backpack. She opened the lid, removed the puff, put the jar up to her lips, and blew the powder in front of her.

As the powder flew through the air, it made the beams of light visible. The girls could now see where all the intersecting laser beams were in the room between the elevator and the vault doors. "Nice!" Hadley took in the effect. "Now how good are you guys at gymnastics?" she asked with a grin.

"Uh . . . I think I can do a somersault?" Isla offered.

"I know some yoga," Blair shared.

"We've got this," Hadley replied. "Just follow me."

Hadley moved her body carefully, leading the girls and Grace over, under, and around the beams. When they were finally across the room, the girls let out a sigh of relief. But there was no time to waste. Blair rushed over to the door and pressed down on the handle. It didn't budge. She was still trying to jiggle the handle when a computerized voice spoke out.

"Please enter your password," the voice announced.

The girls jumped back in surprise. A brightly colored keypad had lit up with numbers on it.

"What would Dame Devin choose?" Hadley wondered.

The computer voice interrupted their thoughts. "Would you like your password hint?"

"Yes!" the girls shouted in unison.

"Your hint is: The Day It All Fell Into Place. You have fifteen seconds before this system locks down."

"What does that mean?" Blair tried to think.

"Ten seconds until system lockdown," the voice replied.

"Wait . . . the day it all fell into place

could mean . . . the day Dame Devin's plan started working," Isla said.

"The day of the car crash!" Blair burst out.

"Five seconds . . . four . . . three . . ." the voice replied.

Blair quickly entered it on the keypad just in time!

"Thank you, Dame Devin!" the voice said as the girls heard a *click* and the vault door opened.

The girls rushed inside and turned on the lights. Blair saw the crown in the center of the room in a protective glass case. She grabbed the glass case.

"How do we get it out of the case?" Grace asked.

"You don't!" an angry voice answered from outside the room. It was Dame Devin!

"Guards!" she yelled. Two palace guards came rushing in and grabbed the case from the girls. "The crown is mine, Blair," Dame Devin snarled. "You'll never be more than a poor lottery girl."

"I *am* more, Dame Devin," Blair said as she pushed against the guard's grip. "And I don't need the crown to prove it."

Dame Devin just laughed. "Good-bye,

Blair. Enjoy Coronation Day." Dame Devin and the guards slammed the heavy vault door behind them. The girls heard Dame Devin resetting the keypad lock, sealing them inside.

Chapter 8

Hours later, Blair, Hadley, and Isla were sitting on the floor in the vault feeling defeated. No matter how hard they had pushed and pulled, they couldn't get the door to open. They were too far underground for their cell phones to work or for anyone to hear them shouting for help. Grace flitted from object to object in the vault, investigating each one and trying not to give up hope while Isla hummed a little tune.

"Wait . . ." said Blair suddenly. "What is that you're humming?"

"Sorry," said Isla sheepishly. "I can't get it out of my head. It's the tune I heard when Dame Devin punched in the new password."

Then Blair had an idea! "Thanks to Isla, we are going to get out of here," Blair said with a huge smile.

With Hadley's help, they removed the back panel of the keypad lock. Then Blair took out her cell phone. She took one of her hairpins and used it to attach the wires from the lock to her cell phone. Now that the phone was linked up with the keypad, they just needed Isla to play the exact same tune of the code Dame Devin punched in to trigger the door to open.

"Isla, I know you can do it!" said Blair encouragingly.

Isla took a deep breath and played the tune on the cell-phone keypad.

The notes were perfect.

The girls heard a click and the vault door slowly popped open.

"Great job, Isla!" Blair exclaimed.

"Go, team!" Hadley said, motioning to the open door.

Inside the grand palace hall, Headmistress Privet and Dame Devin sat at a dais at the front of the room. The coronation ceremony was well under way as the royal judge was crowning a line of princesses with beautiful tiaras from a table beside him and placing one on each student's head.

Finally, only two tiaras and Gardania's

magical crown were left on the table.

Delancy approached the table as slowly as she possibly could. Sooner than she wanted, she was standing right in front of the royal judge.

"Delancy," he stated while picking up the crown, "I now crown you princess of—"

"WAIT!"

Blair, Grace, Hadley, and Isla burst into the room.

Dame Devin leaped out of her chair.

"No! Do NOT wait!" she yelled.

The royal judge and Headmistress Privet exchanged a confused look. What was going on?

"I am making a claim to the throne," Blair called to the crowd. "I am Princess Sophia, daughter of Queen Isabella!"

Everyone in the crowd gasped, except for Dame Devin. She grabbed the magical crown from the royal judge and raced to put it on her daughter's head. But then Delancy tripped her! The crown went flying across the room where Brock stood ready to catch it.

CHOMP!

Prince the dog had leaped into the air and caught the crown in his mouth just as Brock was about to grab it. Prince ran over to Blair where Hadley and Isla quickly

took it from his mouth and placed it on Blair's head.

Before Blair knew it, the crown had begun to glow. Not only did it light up the room but it transformed her uniform into a magnificent coronation ball gown.

"It *is* Princess Sophia!" someone in the crowd yelled.

Dame Devin grabbed her daughter. "You

useless child! I eliminated Queen Isabella so you could be the princess of Gardania!" She was so furious she didn't even realize she had confessed in front of everyone in the crowd.

The royal judge instructed the guards to take Dame Devin to a detention area where the authorities would deal with her.

"Blair . . ." Headmistress Privet said gently once the guards had pulled Dame Devin off the dais. "That is, Princess Sophia . . . let us continue with the coronation ceremony. Is there anything you'd like to say?"

Blair hesitated before taking a few steps forward. Then she smiled confidently and said, "It is strange to be standing here. I'm just a regular girl. But just like Headmistress Privet says—every girl has princess potential. I promise to always work hard . . . and to be fair . . . and to be kind."

Next Blair made sure that Hadley and Isla were crowned princesses and received their tiaras. When it came time for Blair to name her lady royal, she knew just who to pick. "It would be an incredible privilege if you would be my lady royal . . . Delancy," Blair said.

Delancy was shocked. "But . . . but I was horrible to you! Why me?"

"You made it hard for me at first," Blair agreed. "But you made sure to do the right thing when it counted, and I wouldn't be wearing this crown if it weren't for your help."

Delancy looked down. It hadn't been easy, but she had made sure that the truth came out. "I would be honored to be your lady royal . . . Your Highness."

Later that evening, the coronation celebration was in full swing when Blair heard a voice from behind her.

"Congratulations, Princess Blair. Or . . . Sophia?" Prince Nicholas said with a bow.

Blair's eyes lit up and she smiled. "You can still call me Blair," she said.

"Would thou do me the honor of dancing with me?" asked Prince Nicholas as he extended his hand.

Blair gently took his hand. "I would be most delighted."

As the two started for the dance floor, Headmistress Privet approached them. "Your Highness, there are some important people here to see you."

Blair turned toward the door and saw her mother and Emily, who was still wearing her paper tiara. The three of them ran to each other. Blair wrapped her arms around her family.

"Welcome . . . to our new home!" She gestured around her. "I'd like you to meet Headmistress Privet."

"You should be very proud of your princess," Headmistress Privet said to Blair's mother, who blinked back a few happy tears.

Blair beamed. "Come meet my friends."

She was guiding them toward her friends when Emily stopped. "Blair, if you're a princess now . . . does that mean I'm a princess, too?"

Blair stopped and grinned at her sister. She took the paper tiara off her sister's head and replaced it with her own sparkling magical crown.

"Thanks to you, I've learned that there's a princess in *every* girl," she said and put the paper tiara on her own head. "Now let's go! I'll teach you two how to dance!"

And she took her mother's and Emily's hands and led them to the dance floor where Hadley, Isla, and all of her friends were waiting for them.